Pirouli

Aïxa
Sand Castles

Summary of the first book
of the Aïxa collection

*For reasons she found difficult
to understand, Aïxa had to leave her
island of sunshine for a land of snow.
Upon arriving, she is delighted by
so many Christmas trees covered
with twinkling lights of all colors.*

**Also available in
French, Spanish and Italian.**

Aïxa
Snow Castles

Florence Bolté

Mentalo

Pirouli

Text: FLORENCE BOLTÉ
Illustrations: MENTALO
Translation: PHILIP LEE
Graphic design and artistic supervision:
FRANÇOIS ÉMOND
Graphics: CHARLES ST-PIERRE
Collaboration on illustrations, graphic and artistic design:
FLORENCE BOLTÉ
Editing collaboration: CHARLES-HENRI AUDET

My thanks to the Arts Council of Québec, André Leduc,
Djénane Marchand, John Trajan Graves-Marchand
and his friends, Jacques Plessis-Bélair and Robin Simard,
as well as to Manon Arsenault, Dominique Sterlin
and their pupils.

Pirouli publishing house is a division of
ANIMATHON INC.

Pirouli
B.P. 85019
MONT-SAINT-HILAIRE (Québec)
CANADA J3H 5W1
Telephone: (450) 467-8909
E-mail: **pirouli@sympatico.ca**

In the same series:
Sand Castles (Aïxa):
© 2000 Pirouli/**ANIMATHON INC.**

Legal deposit: 2005.
Bibliothèque nationale du Québec.
National Library of Canada.

Printed in Hong Kong.

Library and Archives Canada Cataloguing in Publication

Bolté, Florence

    [Châteaux de neige. English]

    Snow castles

    (Aïxa)
    Translation of: Châteaux de neige.
    Sequel to: Sand castles.
    For children aged 5 and up.

    ISBN 2-922754-05-7

    I. Mentalo. II. Lee, Philip. III. Title. IV. Title:
Châteaux de neige. English. V. Series: Bolté, Florence. Aïxa.

PS8553.O485C42213 2005   jC843'.6 C2005-940247-4
PS9553.O485C42213 2005

To all those who welcomed someone who had to leave his or her country.

To my dear nephews and nieces with their many
nicknames, Raphaël: Ti-tonton, Ti-bilou, Rafifo;
Timothée Gabriel: Gabi, Gabou, Gabilou, TG;
and to Maïa: Maïa di Bahia, Mayaya,
for all the happy times we have shared.

To Oliver Jones, the inspiration for
the character of the young pianist at
the marriage of Uncle Loulou, on page 48.

The moment we arrived at our new apartment from the airport, a beautiful little black cat jumped up at me.

"He's yours, said my Uncle Loulou.
You'll have to give him a name.

— I'll call him Little Cat. No, no, no. I'll call him

Nino!"

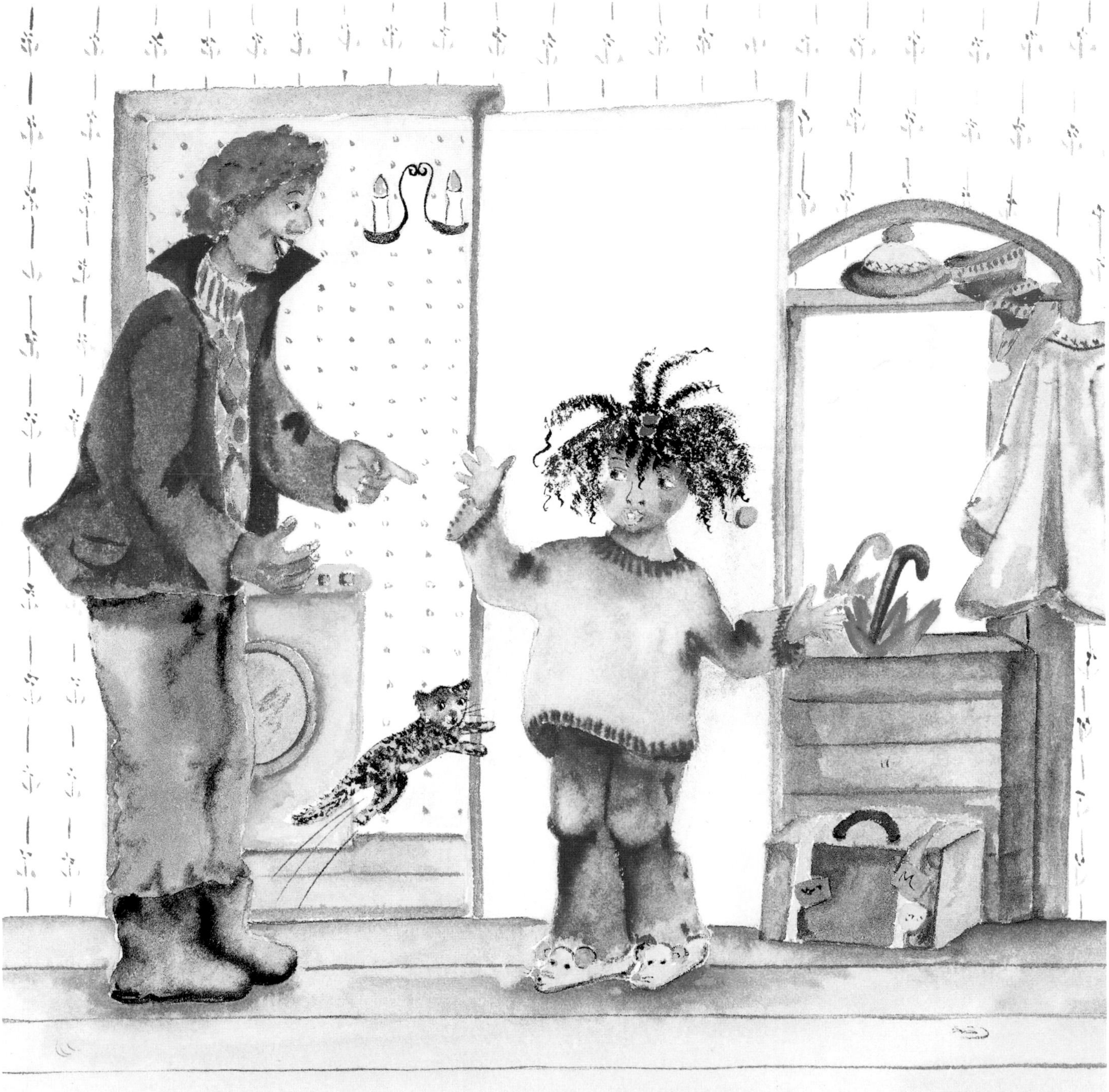

Uncle Loulou took us to visit our apartment, not far from his. There are people living above, below and next to us.

What I like most is the hallway. There's a place where machines swallow coins to wash and dry clothes.

And there's a wonderful smell of apple pie and cinnamon floating in the air.

Hummm!

The day after we arrived, the sun came out!
I didn't think there'd be sunshine in a snowy country.

"Put on your boots and the scarf
the neighbor lent you", said Mommy.

I don't understand why I have to put such heavy objects on my feet
to go outside. It really annoooys me!

"No, no, you have to put your shoes inside the boots.

— Oh, pffffff!

— Come on, Aïxa dear, hurry up! We're going to the church
to find you some winter clothes."

I thought a church was for going to mass or for praying. Here, in the basement of the church, there is a big general store!

I try on clothes, boots, a scarf, a woolen hat and mittens. At last I can go and play outside!

Leaving the church, I dive into the snow. It's like clouds. I stick my nose in. It smells good, it's soft, it's… brrrr! … cold! I laugh. A boy and girl my age come and speak to me. They ask:

"Why are you laughing?

— Snow! Snow's fun! This is the first time I've stuck my nose into snow or touched it. Where I come from, there isn't any snow. It's always hot."

"Do you want to make a snow man or snow castles with us? Oliver asks me.

— Snow castles!"

All afternoon I play with my new friends, Oliver and Nane.

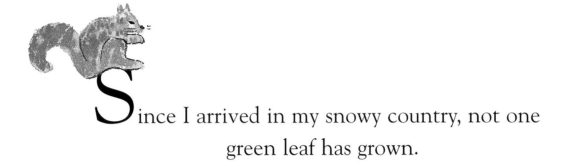

Since I arrived in my snowy country, not one
green leaf has grown.

"Are the trees dead, Daddy?

— They're not dead, Aïxa.
Trees lose their leaves in winter and rest because of the cold.
In spring, they come into bud and the leaves
grow again. In autumn, the leaves
change color and fall.
You'll see, next year.

Have you noticed? Conifers keep their needles in winter."

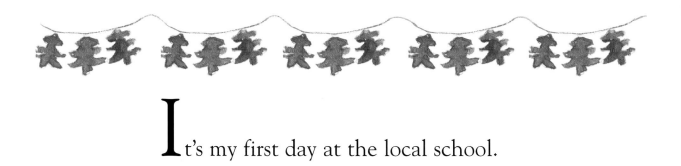

It's my first day at the local school.

Nane and Oliver have come to look for me. In the yard,
the children come up close. They all speak at the same time:

"Can I touch your hair?

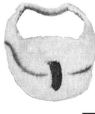

— It's like steel wool.

— Where are you from? You don't talk like us!

— Why are you chocolate colored like that?

— Why is your skin so dark? Did you forget to wash?

— I wash *evwey* day. My skin's that color!"

22

M e, who was so happy to go to school… I cried.

Nicole, my teacher, presented me to the class. I had to say something. So I said "Good mo'ning. I like woses!" All the pupils laughed and replied "Good morrrning!" Nicole gently told me I must pronounce my r's.

At home, in front of the mirror, I repeated the sentences in my school-book: "Cricri will reach for rare roses in Coralie's round garden. The green crocodile rages through the jail bars of his purple cage while crunching rich barley grains.

"Good morrrning! I like roses!"

A week later, no one's laughing at my r's anymore. I pronounce all of them.

At playtime, a boy started teasing me:
"In your country, everyone's lazy, right? You too!"

I looked at him astonished. I was too hurt to cry out:
"You nasty boy! Me, lazy?!"

I may have gotten poor marks in my first exams. I'm tired.
Everything is so new: the snow, the school, the streets, the food, the r's.
I have to get used to so many different things.
But lazy? Never. I'm not a lazybones!

Upset, I told my mom everything.
Mom comforted me and assured me that dad and her loved me a lot,
with my golden caramel skin and my curly hair.

"You know, Aïxa, there are lazy people everywhere,
but no more in our country than anywhere else."

"What about the peasants working in the fields under the blazing sun? The sellers who carry heavy baskets of vegetables on their heads and go on foot from the country to the town? The fishermen who cast their lines for hours in the open sea? Do you really think the people in your country are lazy?

Don't cry, angel, dry your tears…

Work hard at school, show them you're not lazy. And don't forget that it's just one person in the whole school who was mean to you. And above all don't let any more nastiness upset you."

This morning I went to get the mail from our box.
The mailman had just passed.

There is a letter from Grandma.

Mommy opened it and read it to us.

"…Auntie Leah has had a beautiful baby boy:
Nicholas.

Everyone in the village is fine. Aïxa's friend,
Gigi, often asks for news.

Kiki, the little dog, has been pining since you left.
He's thin and sad. We miss you all a lot. Palou is
fine, but he misses his daughter and grand-daughter.
Tomorrow evening there is a party in the village and
we'll be thinking of you three as we celebrate.
Grandma and Palou, with love to all of you."

"Why are you crying, Aïxa? asks mom.

— I… I want to go back to my village with Grandma, Palou,
Gigi and my little dog, Kiki. I don't want to stay here.
It's too cold. And certain kids ask too many questions.
I don't want to pronounce my r's like them. I want to say
good *mo'ning*, eat rice with red beans, vegetables of all colors
and fish. I don't want soft ham sandwiches anymore.
I even miss my godmother Amelia's cow, Lily.
I want to dance, go to school and to the sea
with my friends like before.

— Cry, darling… cry…
say what's in your heart.
It'll do you good…"

I am not as sad as yesterday. I play with my friends Nane and Oliver. We throw snowballs from our open-top snow castles.

"Stop! I don't want to break my glasses, cries Oliver.

— Children! Come and have a snack, says Oliver's grandmother.

— Come and taste the best maple sugar sweets in the world, made by my grandmother, a recipe given to her by her ancestors. She is a Micmac Indian[1], and I call her Granny Micmac, adds Oliver.

— Me too! My name Aïxa is Indian. It comes from the Taïno-Arawak[2] Antilles Indians. My mother told me that the first Aïxa in the land was a cousin of Queen Anacaona…

— A queen in your country? asked Nane.

— Yes, she lived a long time ago. My mother says that even though the Taïnos no longer exist on our island[3], Taïno blood still runs in our veins. From time to time there is an Aïxa in my family so as to remember the Taïnos."

1. The Micmac Indians are among the first inhabitants of North America.
2. The Taïno-Arawak are among the first inhabitants of the West Indies (Antilles).
3. The island Aïxa is referring to carries the Indian names of Haïti, Bohio or Quisqueya, which mean 'Mountainous Land' or 'Great Land'.

Granny Micmac's maple sugar sweets are so good!
They're very much like Grandma's goat's milk toffees.

…American Indian sweets? Of course.

Granny Micmac invites us to eat.
Nane and I telephone our parents to ask
if it's all right. Hurray! They say yes.

The whole evening we told
each other about what
makes us afraid.

Nane told us of her terrible
nightmares. Me, of my fear of
the boogeyman and his sack.
And Oliver of the dreamcatcher
that cured him of his
nightmares.

36

Granny Micmac told us about her favorite things:

"My grandson Oliver's dreamcatcher catches good
and bad dreams. The bad dreams are caught in the net
and burnt up by the first glimmer of dawn. The good
dreams, however, are free and go in and out through
the feathers. I'll give you one too, Nane.
Put it in your bedroom. You'll see…
you'll only have good dreams. Just like Oliver.

To you, Aïxa, I give this little bag made of
kid-leather, with a stone and feathers.

You can put all your fears about the boogeyman
inside. Every time you have a fear, put it in
this protective bag and tie it securely
with this piece of hay.

You'll see. You'll always be protected.

— Thank you, granny Micmac."

After the meal we all went to the living-room, near the fire, and sat on the caribou-skin mat. We played all kinds of riddles and jokes. When my turn came up, I began a Creole riddle where you have to start by saying *"Krik?"* and answer by saying *"Krak!"* if you want to go on.

"What spins around in the sky and looks like lace… and turns into people, animals, boats, castles, houses, fortresses, geometric shapes or storms?"

Despite the clues, Nane and Oliver thought for a long time without finding the answer. Finally, it was granny Micmac who said:

"Come on, children… it's snow!"

I feel really happy with Nane, Oliver, and granny Micmac's stories.

The following day, Sunday, we go to the mountains with Uncle Loulou and his fiancée, Clara. It's so cold we take a taxi.

The driver speaks French and Creole like us. I don't understand everything he says, but I think he too has had problems being accepted. Like me, at school, with my dark skin, my curly hair and my r's.

On the lake everyone is skating. It's ever so niiiiiice!

People look like snow-stars on a mirror.

The boys and girls hold hands and make circles and patterns on the ice with their skates. I'd like to go skating with my friends.

For now, with my boots, I trace a huge snowman with a hat in the snow. A real giant. It's great fun to play in the snow.

In the mountains, people ski down the slopes
and children slide on sleds.

On the river, there are long-distance skiers. One of them is being
pulled by a little dog. Others are wearing snow-shoes.

"Aïxa, would you like to do winter sports? asked Uncle Loulou.

— With Kiki… Nino and my friends… I'd love to!

— Come on then, the whole lot of you, come and slide on a sled,
said Uncle Loulou.

— I'll watch you first and go next!"

Ah, they go so faaaaaast!

"Your turn, Aïxa!" Clara says.

42

Good news! I got the best marks in class for math!
I don't know if it's because my teacher congratulated me,
but this week more children are playing with me at break-time.
I get on very well with Cloclo. She's nice.

After school I walk home with Cloclo.
I'm glad I've got her as a friend in my class.

We chatted about her skating and sliding games, her snow castles,
my games at the seaside, my sand castles, fish of many colors,
fishermen's boats, and our friends.

When she left for the Christmas vacation, she said,
"One day we'll go skating together, or sledding!"

"Hurry up, Aïxa, we mustn't be late for Uncle Loulou's wedding," said Mommy.

There's snow everywhere, on the fir-trees, on the river and even on the church steps.

The bride is beautiful. And her husband too. They are the color of milk and chocolate.

I am one of the bridesmaids.

47

At the party
the musicians are setting
the mood. Uncle Oliver
is fantastic on the piano.
Almost without stopping
I dance Creole dances
and some from here.

The smell of rice, red beans and
barbecued chicken entices me.
Everything smells good and delicious!
And the wedding cake! Mmmmm!!

Uncle Loulou looks like he's in love.
He never stops looking at Aunt Clara.
He whispers sweet nothings
in her ear. Me, I dance with
the children and especially
with Leo. He's eight.

A few days after Uncle Loulou and aunt Clara's wedding,
I went to see Santa Claus. He smells like chocolate, Santa Claus,
doesn't he? And he looks like he enjoys his food.

"Ho, ho, ho! What do you want for Christmas,
my pretty Aïxa? A doll?

— Er... No.

— Then what would you like?

— I'd like... I'd like a little brother!"

Looking at my mom and dad, Santa Claus said:

"Next year for certain you'll have a little brother or sister.
Have you thought of anything else?

— Skates!

— Be good, Aïxa, and Santa Claus will give you
a lovely surprise. Ho, ho, ho!"

At last Christmas Eve has come! Our Christmas tree sparkles with different colors. Two days before Christmas we decorated it like we do in my sunny country. As we wait for Christmas Eve dinner, I write to Grandma, Palou, Gigi and Gabou.

My tree and the turkey,
they smell so gooooood!

Before going to bed, we sing Creole songs.

I also prepare a little cup of hot chocolate with cookies for Santa Claus. Outside there's a blizzard. I hope he still comes, he has so many homes to visit! Good night, Daddy! Good night, Mommy!

I dream about all the people I love in my village: Grandma, Palou, my godmother Amelia, aunt Leah, Uncle Camille, Gigi, Gabou, my cousin Nicholas and Kiki. They, too, are celebrating Christmas.

Toc, toc, toc, toc. Bing, bang, bada bang. Klak!

A door banging and the strong wind
wake me. I run to the kitchen.
Ahhhh! My biscuits have gone!
And someone drank the chocolate!

I knew Santa Claus liked chocolate!

Santa Claus is already far away.
I can barely see him in the blizzard.
His reindeer and sled have been
carried away by the snowstorm.
I can't see anything now.

In bed, with Nino, I dream about snow castles, sand castles, the sea, the color blue and little Santa Claus going round the world.

Good night Mommy and Daddy. Good night Grandma and Palou.

Good night Kiki and Nino… Good night everyone!

I love you all and I love my two countries!

Zzzzzzzzzzzzzzzzzzzzzzzzzzz…

Kwen-kwen

1. Follow the dots and cut out the game square, on page 59.

2. Fold the square in two,

   then
   in four.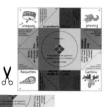

3. Open the square.

   Fold each corner over
   to the centre and join
   the following numbers:
   1 towards 5
   2 towards 6
   3 towards 7
   4 towards 8

4. Turn the square
   round

   and fold each of the triangles
   AA, BB, CC and DD

   towards the white dot in the
   centre, to form a
   smaller square.

5. Fold the small square in
   two. The tips of the
   triangles must point towards
   the inside of the game.

6. Slide your thumbs and index fingers under each of the animal
   or object illustrations (1 to 4),
   making sure that the tips of the little
   cones point upwards. Move the toy
   until it feels easy in your hands.

The game   (You can play alone or with a partner.)

1. To start the game, call out the Creole word **Kwen-kwen?**
   (Pronounced **kwan-kwan**.)
   The player, if he or she wants to play,
   must make a sign or say **Kwen!**

2. Tell the player to choose a word relating to one
   of the animals or objects.

   (2.1 Variations: Ask the player to choose a number
   between 1 and 10; or a color.)

3. Spell the animal's or object's name and move your thumb
   and index finger backwards and forwards for each
   letter of the chosen name.

   (3.1 Variations: Count up to the number
   chosen or spell out the color chosen while moving
   your fingers the right number of times.)

4. Ask the player to point to a colored triangle in the mouth
   of the **Kwen-kwen**, and ask the question you see there.

5. Check the answer by lifting up the fold.

6. Start the game over as many times
   as you want and, from time to time,
   try variations (see 2.1 and 3.1).

   If you're finished playing, look for more suggestions
   in the circle at the centre of the large square.

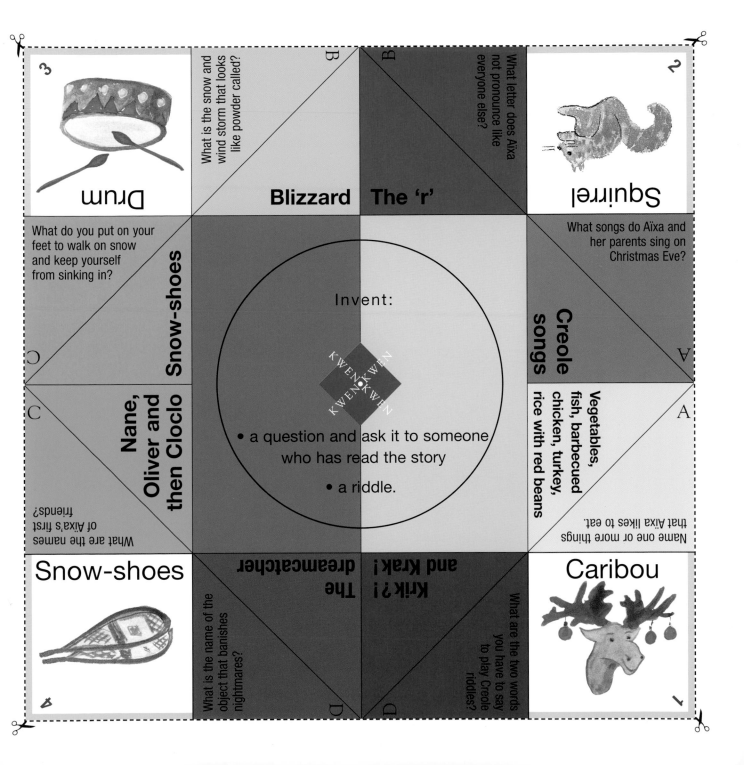

3 Drum

B — What is the snow and wind storm that looks like powder called? **Blizzard**

B — What letter does Aïxa not pronounce like everyone else? **The 'r'**

2 Squirrel

What do you put on your feet to walk on snow and keep yourself from sinking in? **Snow-shoes**

A — What songs do Aïxa and her parents sing on Christmas Eve? **Creole songs**

Invent:
- a question and ask it to someone who has read the story
- a riddle.

KWEN·KWEN

O — C

Snow-shoes 4

What is the name of the object that banishes nightmares? **The dreamcatcher**

Krik?! and krak! — What are the two words you have to say to play Creole riddles?

Caribou 1

Name one or more things that Aïxa likes to eat. **Vegetables, fish, barbecued chicken, turkey, rice with red beans** — A

What are the names of Aïxa's first friends? **Nane, Oliver and then Cloclo** — C

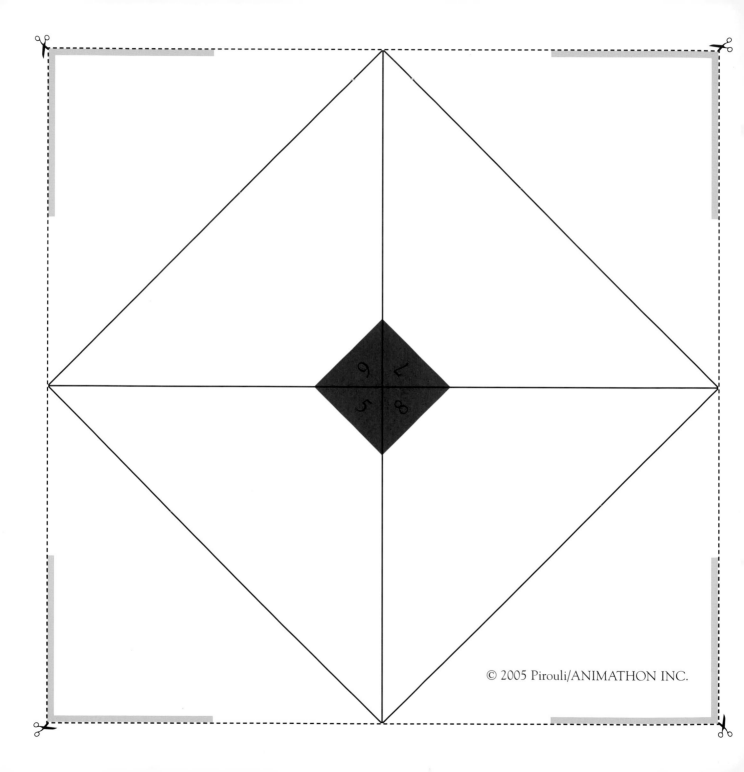

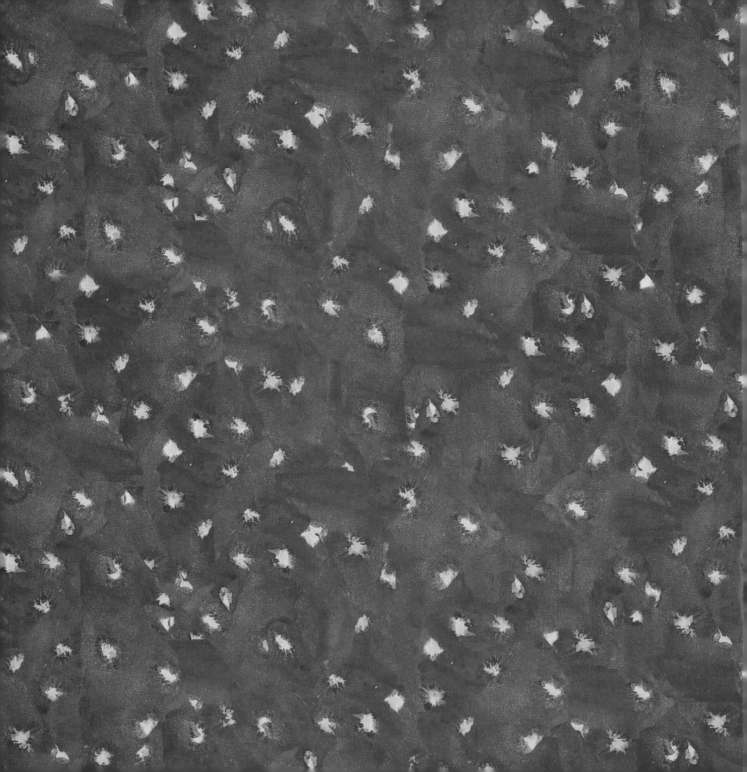